INDECENTLY THICK

Straight to Gay MM First Time

Michael Levi

ISBN: 9798803819691
Imprint: Independently published

2nd edition

Cover design by: Michael Levi

CONTENTS

CHAPTER 1

As a married man who just had my second gay experience, I was longing for more. My first time was with Mike, a gay cop who kept his true sexual orientation hidden. My second time was with my Dutch friend, and the worst was that not everything happened according to my expectations.

Donny, in the end, decided to stay with his cheating girlfriend. I couldn't believe the words that came out of his mouth when he explained his decision to stay with Danica.

"Are you FUCKING serious?!" I asked crustily at him.

"Yeah... You know better than anyone how much I love her, Lucas. What we did that night... it was just an experience."

"But I just can't forget it!"

"Lucas... don't you have a wife to go back to?" He asked before closing the door in front of me and leaving me alone in the hallway.

Daisy? FUCK HER. She's probably humping several men in a gangbang. I want you, Donny. When will you finally understand that?

Not only was Donny a good-looking Dutchman, but he was also kind and shy. I had a soft spot for people with low self-esteem like him. Plus, that accent of his... OH MY GOD, I couldn't stop thinking about him!

I was going crazy, especially because Daisy had called saying she wanted me to come back. I said, "Honey, NO. I'm not going back. I know you have already betrayed me multiple times. Truth is, I already did that to you. So yeah, it's better to end this. We should prepare the paperwork and never see each other again."

She then hung up on me and the next time we were supposed to meet would be to make the divorce official. I was kind of content that she didn't say anything else, too. As far as I was concerned, Daisy wasn't my wife anymore.

Anyhow, my biggest concern was Donny. I was pretty sure his girlfriend was cheating on him. I just needed to find solid proof – more solid than her online messages – to make Donny finally break up with her.

I had a special power that allowed me to shrink my body to any size I wanted. I used that power to spy on Donny when he was taking a shower, sleeping, using his computer, playing games, fucking Danica, etc. In other words, I was a camera constantly aimed at him.

I could use that power to get the proof I wanted, but even with that in my favor, finding what I needed would be a challenge. I'd have to find where Danica lived and stalk her until she met up with her lover.

Then, with my phone in hand, I'd take pictures and record her cheating on Donny. That would be all the proof I needed. I was very excited to start my plan.

Meanwhile, I would have to content myself with spying on Donny. Of course, he didn't know about my superpower. Nobody could find that about me because I'd be all over in the news. It was a gift given to me that required responsibility.

It was about midnight when I went to Donny's room in the apartment building. We both lived downtown, and I somewhat expected him to be already sleeping because of his morning classes.

To my surprise, the light in his bedroom was turned on. I was so small that I could use the gap between the door and the floor to go to him.

Donny wasn't playing games on his computer as I imagined he would be. He was sitting on his bed, stark naked and stroking his giant cock gently while using his phone.

I carefully made my way so that I could see what it was that he was seeing on his phone. Danica? Oh yeah, of course that the hopeless Dutch lover was jacking off to her pictures.

To be honest, she was a hottie. The problem was that she was also a BITCH. A big, hot BITCH that didn't care about Donny. I didn't know why she just didn't dump him, but either way, it infuriated me.

From where I was, only a couple of centimeters from Donny's head and huge back, I could take in all the details of his hot body.

He was a cute, blond Dutchman with an athletic body capable of making most men feel envy. I knew I was envious of him. I was kind of similar to him physically, with the biggest difference being the color of my dirty blond hair.

I was also about fifteen years older than he was, and at my age, I already had some wrinkles on my face. Donny had the face of someone even much younger than he was. He was so dreamy.

I stood in awe watching his hand going up and down on his huge cock. He was circumcised and his cockhead was crimson red. I remembered that night when I sucked him off. I wished nothing more than to be able to do the same every day.

Before long, Donny put his phone aside, closed his eyes, and started to jack off vigorously. I had already lowered my pants and was yanking myself off while admiring him, who was like a Greek god.

In a matter of seconds, he blew his load on his well-worked, almost fat-free abdomen. At the same time, I also released my hot cum on the surface of his bed support.

He used some tissue paper to clean his belly and then quickly turned off the light before falling asleep. I then walked out of his bedroom and went back to mine. I was very excited to put my plan into action and catch Danica in the act.

CHAPTER 2

I used my special power to find some documents in Donny's house which contained Danica's address. She had left a couple of water and electricity bills for him to pay – poor man! – and I used that information to start my plan.

I decided to use some old clothes to blend in with the rest of the city. I grabbed my very reliable phone and headed out. Danica's place was about twenty minutes from downtown, so it wasn't going to take me long to get there.

I took the metro to get to her house. It was Saturday, so she wasn't supposed to have classes. I knew she would probably be there. I didn't know if she would meet her lover, but on an overcast Saturday, why would she be spending the whole day in her house?

Donny had said to me they wouldn't meet each other that day, and I believed him. He never once lied to me. He was a little annoyed that I always brought up Danica, but he wasn't suspicious that anything was up.

Danica lived on the outskirts of the main part of the city. The neighborhood was fairly middle-class. There were some poor houses here and there, but the location was mostly pleasant.

My plan was to shrink and spy on her for the whole day to collect data. The proof I was looking for would eventually come because I knew she was betraying Donny.

She did provide my Dutch friend with a bullshit explanation

that only a desperate guy like him could believe. All I knew was that I was determined to make the man see the light of day.

It was about 10 AM when I reached her place. Her house was as average as any other in the neighborhood. There were no walls, so I had no difficulty using the gap in her door to enter it.

She lived with her parents, but they weren't home. I knew they wouldn't come soon, which meant that the probability of her lover coming there was relatively high.

I made my way to her bedroom, which had the door open. The young woman was on the bed and using her phone. When I climbed up her bedsheets and the support of her bed, I found out that she was checking out a man's photo collection.

Ah, so that's her lover! I thought before a message notification popped up on the screen of her phone.

From where I stood, I could perfectly read what it said, "Honey, are you available today?"

"Sure. Care to come here? My parents are out for the day."

"Perfect. I'm going, then. Kisses. Love you."

"I love you too."

So, there it was... that was the man she was having an affair with. I was fuming! That BITCH was BETRAYING MY Donny and he was still acting like she cared about him.

I grabbed my phone and made sure that the camera was working. Everything was going according to my expectations. All I needed to do now was to remain hidden and record the two of them together.

The lover of Danica, Jeremy, had come and he used the doorbell to call the bitch. She hopped off the bed and ran to the front door to open it. I hurried over there to see what the man was like in person.

He was easily a lot taller than I was, relatively skinny for a man of his height, had black and thick hair, a nicely maintained beard, and brown eyes. He wore casual clothes and a pair of flip-flops.

Danica proceeded to hug her lover and bring him closer to her. He put his big, masculine hands on her lower back and kissed the bitch on her lips.

Even though I hated both of them, I couldn't deny that seeing them like that was turning me on. I felt my small dickie growing harder and bigger against the fabric of my boxer briefs.

Then, I slapped myself on the face to make sure I wasn't going to forget why I was here. It hurt, but it served to put my mind back in the right place.

"You look so hot today", Jeremy murmured into Danica's ear. The woman trembled under the warmth of his words.

I quickly grabbed my phone and started to record their next lines.

"You too, my love. You too…", she cooed before giving the man another kiss on his lips and inviting him into her bedroom.

Damn, they were going to start early, I thought. They made their way to her bedroom and both were in no hurry to get there. A crispy-clear romantic atmosphere surrounded them.

I knew I already had the proof I needed at that moment. There was no way Donny could deny that Danica didn't love him. However, I couldn't leave her house right now, either. I wanted to see the two of them having sex. I was naughty like that.

Danica started to slowly undress the tall man in front of her. There was a clear look of lust on their faces that turned me on even more than I was.

Without the clothes, Jeremy wasn't sexually appealing to me. Still, I was a sucker for guys, so I still fancied him.

Once Danica had taken his boots and pants off, she traced her tongue across his abdomen and gave him a couple of kisses on his fat nipples.

Then, the tall man used his two masculine hands to take her clothes off. Danica was wearing a yellow bra and panties.

Then, she fell over on the bed and said with a clearly high-pitched voice, "Will you take care of me and change my diaper?"

"Sure, I will", he said before putting his hands on the bed for support and kissing his lover again.

I couldn't believe what I was seeing! They were going to do some kind of kinky play where one would pretend to be the caretaker and the other, an annoying little. It was the ABDL kink that I loved a lot. My cock grew even harder instantly at the thought of watching those two roleplaying like that!

Jeremy, then, grabbed his cock and offered it to Danica, who sat on the bed and carefully wrapped her lips around it. Jeremy was hairier than most men commonly were, which was a bit of a turn-on.

Danica bobbed up and down on his cock as if she was sucking a bottle of milk. Sometimes, she would behave as if she was sucking a breast full of the same stuff. She knew what she was doing and had probably already done that many times before!

Then, it hit me: was she with Jeremy because Donny didn't want to pretend to be her caretaker? Maybe that was the case, since I never saw Donny doing that to Danica.

Well, it was okay that she had an itch that needed to be scratched, but nothing could explain her betrayal of my Dutch friend.

I grabbed my phone and recorded more of the action. I wonder what else, other than to ditch that bitch, Donny would think while he watched the recording. Did he know about that weird side of Danica?

Regardless, those questions were for later. I put my phone back inside my pocket and watched the two of them continue doing what they were doing.

Danica was now sucking on his dick and loving it with her mouth. She never went farther than his head, showing her fear of gagging.

Then, once she was tired of that, she took his cock out and offered Jeremy to put the diaper on her. She opened her legs for him, her hairy pussy now glistening with desire, while she bit gently one of her fingers. Her eyes looked demanding as she said, "Will you take care of me and put the diaper on, pretty please?"

Jeremy walked slowly toward the cabinet and opened a drawer. Then, he grabbed a petite geriatric diaper and walked back to Danica.

He carefully placed the diaper on her and kissed her hairless legs from top to bottom. Danica responded by groaning and moaning softly.

Meanwhile, I was stroking my cock slowly while I enjoyed what they were doing. Ahhh, if only they weren't cheating on Donny, I'd be thinking that they were like two cute cupids.

Then, Danica slid off the bed and started to crawl around in the bedroom. She was even making some weird sounds like babbling and pretending to cry. Jeremy smiled and showed that he approved of what she was doing. He had his cock in his hand and was stroking it slowly.

Then, he mounted on her and demanded, "Take me for a spin, sugar!" And his lover did as she was told. She left the bedroom and walked all over the house while carrying Jeremy on her back. *Good thing he wasn't heavy,* I joked.

I stayed where I was because I had a good view of them. Danica crawled about in the living room, then back to her bedroom, and then to the kitchen. They were so taken by their play that they never noticed me!

I grabbed my phone again and recorded more of their silly roleplay. I knew Donny would eventually laugh his ass off years later after breaking up with that bitch.

Jeremy was slapping his lover on the butt and inciting her to keep going. Not once did Danica look like she wasn't enjoying that. Quite the contrary: it seemed to me she wanted that moment to last forever.

Then, they eventually came back to the bedroom and Jeremy grabbed some clothes that were too small for Danica. He helped to put them on her and, then, she lied down and offered her glistening pussy for him.

Jeremy lied down on top of her and started to kiss her whole body. He went from her feet to her legs, then to her lips and the region around her flower, then to her abdomen before finally stopping at her lips. The sound of their kisses was like music to my ears.

While Danica was fully clothed, Jeremy wasn't. His cock and balls were pressing against her body and looking readier, as the seconds passed, to devour her. Danica would push them aside a bit to tell him to wait a bit more.

Meanwhile, Jeremy was a bit pissed that she wanted to take things slow. He kept guiding his cock to her pussy and pressing it even harder against her. Since her panties were too small, there were times when his dong would push them aside a bit and touch her warm cunt.

"C'mon, honey. Let's do that thing, too", Danica pleaded while pointing to her kitchen table. They had a chair that she wanted to sit on and pretend that she wasn't a grown woman anymore.

"Anything you want, sugar", Jeremy growled while picking her up and slowly bringing her to the kitchen. He settled her on the chair, then she grabbed a pair of spoons and demanded that he brought her some food.

"I wanth food! I wanth food!" She continuously repeated while punching the table with the spoons in her hands.

"I'm on it! Just wait a bit", the naked man said before going to the fridge. He whipped up porridge for her, and it smelled nice. She ate all of it quickly and looked at her lover.

"I wanth miww now! I wanth miww now!" Danica said while punching the table again.

Jeremy, then, went to the fridge and grabbed a bottle before filling it with some milk. Danica drank the cold liquid in one go and said, "I wanth tho shweep now! I wanth tho shweep now!"

Yet again, Jeremy picked her up in his arms and carried the woman to the bedroom. I hadn't left the place I was at and continued recording the whole thing, so I had a favorable view of when he laid her belly up on the bed.

"I don'th wiwe thhish thhing on me anymore…" Danica said before Jeremy readied himself to take her diaper off. The woman lifted her legs up a bit to make it easy for him, and in a matter of seconds, her pussy was already exposed again.

Jeremy, then, shot his hand to her cunt and started to caress it. Danica rested her head on the bed and started to moan in pleasure.

She had her eyes closed and seemed to be enjoying the moment a lot!

Meanwhile, even I was surprised that I was managing to last that long without blowing my load all over the surface of their bed's support. Minutes had already passed since they started role-playing like that. I wondered when it would end.

"Don't you think you need to sleep now, sweetheart?" Jeremy said while grabbing her legs and bringing the woman closer to him.

"Now now?" She asked with a very innocent look on her face.

"Yes, now now", he responded while sniffing her pussy.

"Okay", she said while forcing him to come closer to her. His cock was now pressing against the opening of her cunt and threatening to breach it.

It was then that I realized that Jeremy's manhood was nothing to be ashamed of. It was about the same length as Donny's and incredibly thick. I was drooling as I thought about sucking it. *Maybe, if circumstances were different, I could be devouring it...*

Danica lifted her knees up and offered, yet again, her glistening pussy for the hungry brat. He looked like a proper college young man, and maybe he was even a classmate of hers. It was possible that Donny was someone he knew. *So, that meant extra problems for my Dutch friend after he discovered what she has been doing with Jeremy.*

Jeremy climbed up on the bed, put his two hands on her thick thighs, and guided his big man tool into her pussy. Danica looked at him and then down before widening her mouth and eyes in complete awe!

Jeremy then put just a small section of his dong inside of her. I could clearly see his dong penetrating her and forcing the muscles of her cunt to adapt to his man tool.

Then, slowly and carefully, he slid the rest of his big dong inside her. She emitted a long and loud groan of pleasure when he was fully inside her. She used her legs around his back to force even more of him in her! What a beast that woman was!

Then, Jeremy started to pound her slowly. He was sliding in

and out of her without a condom. *Did… they forget that?* It was possible, given that they weren't thinking straight right now.

Either way, I considered that if she was to get pregnant or an STD, it would make my job a lot easier! Donny wouldn't want anything to do with her again if he found out that she was carrying the baby of another man in her.

The only downside was that I wouldn't be able to suck his hot cum like I did with Donny's. Ahhhh… and just thinking about my friend's man milk already made me feel thirsty to taste him again! I could barely wait for the two cupids to be done for the day so that I could go back home!

Jeremy, then, started to pound the young woman fervently! I was in awe as I watched the pure and raw strength he had. He wasn't just ramming Danica – he was devouring her alive!

Danica was moaning and groaning like the bitch she was. I was recording all of that with my phone while still stroking my cock. *Donny will love it when he watches it*, I thought.

"OH JEN, JUST FUCK ME. FUCK ME HARDER", she kept on saying to her lover. The words only found deaf ears since he was completely focused on what he was doing. The beast wasn't even blinking while he ravaged her pussy!

Then, he finally reached his climax. I noticed his whole body stiffening while his balls and cock got ready to blow all his load inside her.

Before the worst could happen to Danica, though, he soon pulled out and aimed his cock at her face. Danica was taken by surprise when she opened her eyes and one spurt of his man milk came roaring through the air before hitting the upper side of her cheek.

One after the other, more spurts of his hot milk coated her face! He was holding his cock in his hand while trying to keep it under control. It looked that he hadn't fapped in quite a while, given how copious his load was.

He emitted one last and long groan of pleasure as the last spurt came out and hit the woman's upper lip. She had the face of someone who didn't expect that.

"Oh Jen, you are SOOOO tasty!" Danica said loudly while using her hand to lick his hot cum on her face. The sticky glob was so warm that her white face was now all red-ish.

Meanwhile, I finally blew my cum and proceeded to sit a bit to relax while the two cupids went to sleep. I was gasping for air due to having endured that very energetic moment alongside the bitch and her lover.

Minutes later, I put my pants on and headed out. That was a job well done and I had all the evidence I needed. *Donny will surely dump her now*, I thought.

CHAPTER 3

When I got back home, it was already close to one in the morning, so I thought it would be better to send the video to Donny tomorrow. I was also tired, so I really had no motivation to pester him at that time.

When I got up, the first thing I did was to send him the video. I created a completely fake email for that since I didn't want him to find out that I had spied on his girlfriend.

After that, all I needed to do was to wait. He would eventually see her again, and I'd know when he ended his relationship with her by watching Danica storming out through the hallway. *That will be a joy to watch!* I thought.

"Donny, I swear it wasn't me!" I heard Danica shouting from the other side of the hallway before rushing down the stairs.

Great, that means he finally broke up with that BITCH. HAHAHAHA I can't wait to have him all for myself, I thought before putting on some fancy clothes and spraying cologne.

Then, I hopped down the hallway and knocked on his door. He immediately opened it and had a fake smile on his face to pretend that everything was dandy.

If I didn't know better, I would have believed him.

"Donny, is everything alright?" I asked while checking him out from bottom to top. He was wearing nothing more than his white shorts. *Oh, those nipples look so damn big today!* I thought while salivating with my mouth.

"Yeah, I'm… okay. I just broke up with Danica. I found out about something really awful she did. Anyway, do you want to come in?"

"Sure, whatever I can do to make you feel better…"

This time, Donny decided not to sit on his couch and offer me some drinks. He went to his bedroom, sat on the bed, and asked me to sit beside him, which I did.

Then, he picked up his phone and played the video I had sent him.

"Do you see this? It's Danica and she was cheating on me with another man! Can you believe that?! Someone recorded the whole thing and sent it to me. I don't know who it was, but that's the least of my worries right now."

"Oh, it's terrible, Donny. I can't believe she was cheating on you!"

"Yep, and the worst is that I don't know what I'll do from now on. I… loved her a lot."

"Well, you have other people who care about you."

"Huh? Like you? Look, Lucas, I know we had that night together, but that was just two friends helping each other out through a difficult moment, right?"

"Do you really think that it was all it was?"

Donny, then, didn't reply straight away. He continued to look at me, maybe trying to figure out what I had meant by those last words. I had a serious look on my face and I didn't plan on changing it.

Shortly afterward, my Dutch friend put his phone aside and kissed me on the lips. There was no warning or anything like that. He just decided to open himself for me right then and there.

"I'm glad you finally get it, Donny", I said before kissing him back.

Then, we started making out vigorously. I forced him to lie down on his back on the bed while using my hands to caress his body.

Ah, I've wanted to touch him like this ever since that night when I gave him that blowjob! The man had such a soft and tender body that I just couldn't have enough of it!

My tongue was dancing and fighting against his for domination. Our lips were rubbing against each other vigorously while he caressed my back with his hands.

Then, he took off my shirt so that he could better love my back. I could feel his warm hands going from one side to the other. The touch of his fingers against my skin was so good I even had goosebumps!

"Oh Donny, you are so FUCKING HOT", I murmured into his ear before kissing his neck. The taste and softness of his body were something like no other I had seen in my life.

Then, I took off my pants and underwear to better appreciate the moment. Donny followed suit and was now also fully naked. Our cocks were rock-hard and standing proudly against each other.

Then, without needing an invitation, I dropped to my knees and sniffed his cock. I gave it some quick kisses as a way to show him my pure appreciation. Donny was looking down and had a very satisfying smirk across his cute face.

Afterward, I slowly wrapped my lips across his big and red cockhead. *Ah! I missed this so much!*

The feeling of my lips against his cockhelmet was nothing short of magnificent. It kept on turning me on and making me feel even more lust. I just wanted to keep on devouring this delicious thing!

It was at that moment that the unexpected happened. I began to shrink and shrink some more slowly. I thought that his dick was getting bigger, but it was my secret that was being revealed.

"Err… Lucas, what's going on?" Donny said with a clear look of shock on his face.

"I'm sorry. You shouldn't be seeing this."

"Huh?"

"Donny… I have a gift. It's something hard to wrap your head around, but basically, I can shrink to any size."

Donny was gawking and I couldn't blame him for that. It didn't seem that he was getting what I was trying to explain.

And thus, I added, "I can shrink to any size, and I guess it can be kind of helpful in some situations. Now, will you please keep this secret?"

Donny continued gawking at me before nodding slowly. Good! I trusted him to keep that a secret.

"Now that's out, can you use your power now?"

His look of confusion changed to that of naughtiness. *What dirty plan is he concocting in his mind?* I asked myself.

"Let me think…" I said before becoming so small that even his cock was bigger than me. I was on top of it and looking up at its owner.

Donny seemed even more excited at that moment. Maybe he was finally having glimpses of what could be done with my superpower.

I walked towards his cockhead and hugged it passionately. My face was connected to it and the smell of musk that was coming from him was stronger than ever.

Then, I decided to please a sexual desire I had, which was to hug a man much bigger than I was. Donny was about the same height I was, so up until then, I hadn't been able to scratch that itch.

I grew back so that I was a head shorter than Donny. I proceeded to hug him passionately and bury my head in his strong chest. Ahhhh! That feeling was just soooo good. I wanted to stay like this until the end of time.

Shortly afterward, I got down to my knees and wrapped my lips around his red cockhead. Since my mouth was smaller, I had to widen my lips a lot more so that I could cherish his meaty manhood.

The whole feeling was a lot different than the first time I sucked him off. I was struggling so much and yet it was so worth it.

I kept on sucking his big man tool for a couple of minutes. His powerful instrument was almost too much for me to handle. Even against such an obstacle, I still managed to please this demanding young man.

The next thing I thought that would be hot to do at the moment was to have him penetrate my smaller asshole. *Could we do it?* I asked myself. The difference in size was considerable, but if we managed to pull it off, the experience would be unforgettable.

I got up to my feet, caressed his round chin, and said, "Do you want to fuck me?"

"Fuck yeah, that's what I've been thinking, Lucas", he murmured while readying his cock. A smart young man like him knew what that truly meant.

I carefully put my elbows on his desk and offered my butt for him. It was wide open for his blue eyes to feast on. He approached me casually and started to caress my asscheeks.

Then, I said, "Just so you know, I'm clean."

"Perfect", he said before grabbing the bottle of lube and putting it beside me. He wanted to take things slow, so he started by licking my asshole and wetting it.

The feeling of his tongue against the skin of my orifice was magical! Ahhhh, I wished we could be doing this all day long.

Then, my Dutch friend opened the bottle of lube and spread some of it on his hand. He gracefully lubed up his enormous cock before doing the same to my frightened orifice.

He even used two fingers to get my rectum oiled up. Then, he went to the drawer and got a package of condoms. I watched him slowly put the condom on his cock and move back to where I was.

Shortly afterward, I felt the head of his cock pressing against my butthole. Just as I had imagined, the difference in size was too big. Much as he tried, Donny couldn't penetrate me.

But then, out of nowhere, he managed to pierce through! I felt my asshole being torn apart by his rigid member and coming inside effortlessly. Once the initial and most difficult barrier was broken through, nothing could stop him anymore!

He put more and more inches inside me before starting to pound me. I felt his veiny manhood coming in and out with almost no friction as the seconds passed.

I was burning hot. My sweat was pooling on his table and making it difficult for me to stand still. Donny was having a very similar problem, since he even had to grab me by the waist for support.

Seconds later, he finally blew his load inside me, or rather, inside the condom. I felt his hot liquid filling the plastic before he slid out his member one last time.

He took out the condom full of cum and I went down to my knees to beg, "Donny... Can I have it?"

"Sure", he said before dropping the condom. I snatched it midair with a winning smile plastered on my face.

Donny, then, sat on his bed and watched as I swallowed the content of his condom. It certainly turned him on again, noticing his cock springing back up.

CHAPTER 4

Donny did indeed break up with Danica for good. Never again did they meet or try to contact each other. He seemed a happier man, which in turn made me happier as well. I always kind of felt I was responsible for him.

Our relationship only grew stronger from then on. We weren't just friends anymore; he was my boyfriend! I even started going to college again just to have the same classes he did.

As for my superpower... Donny eventually got what it truly meant. We started to make use of it for some useful purposes, and also to create more imaginative sex plays.

I never thought I'd find myself in love with another man, but there I was, thinking about marrying Donny. I couldn't wait until that day came...

The End

Find the other books of this series below. They're all straight to gay, first time stories.

1. On His Knees
2. Privately Shared
4. Bicurious Troubles
5. Size Matters

6. Reduced to Nothing

Leave a review if you liked the book. It always helps me so much!

TEASER: ON HIS KNEES

Straight to Gay MM First Time Cheating and Shameless - 1

My neighbor, Mike, was on the other side of the street when he requested my help in order to relocate some dirt that was on his backyard. It was a relatively warm Sunday afternoon, and since I liked being the perfect and proactive neighbor, I crossed the street as I accepted his request.

Meanwhile, my wife was supposed to be at her cousin's place to spend the night and help him with his computer, which had broken down recently. She worked as a computer repair specialist, and since they were good friends, she didn't even demand a payment.

I was planning on using the weekend to watch some naughty movies in my man cave and jack myself off, since my wife recently refused to have sex with me during the last couple of days.

My neighbor had moved in recently and I found out that he worked as a police officer. He was very tall, easily a head taller than I was, aged about 30, extremely hairy with muscles that could excite envy from any man. I knew I was envy of his near perfect athletic body.

I took off my jean pants in order to put on some shorts, work boots, and a white tank top before crossing the street. We moved dirt from one spot to the other for about three hours under a very hot sun. We were both sweating like pigs, and I liked that.

When we finished relocating the dirt, it was about five in the afternoon. Mike said thanks before offering to buy a pizza and ice-cold cans. He also said that I could use the hot tub, which I was glad to accept as well. The day had been a tiresome one, and at that time, all I wanted was to relax.

His bathtub was located in his backyard, and since huge walls closed off his whole house, we could have some much-needed privacy there. Since his plan to relax looked good, I informed him I just needed to go back to my house in order to grab a towel before returning there.

Just as I was about to get there, the doorbell on the other side of the street hanged, which meant the pizza guy had already come. *That was fast!* Mike, then, shouted from his house for me to hurry up if I didn't want the pizza to get cold.

Since my wife did not like doing the laundry often, I could not find a pair of briefs for me to wear. I decided that was the least of my worries, since I could ask Mike to lend me one. Thus, I headed back to his place. There, he offered me to go upstairs to his room to grab one of his briefs, which I was glad to accept. They were all white, and I found that somewhat curious.

As I fumbled through his briefs, I managed to find one that was just about my waist size. I grabbed it and quickly put in on. I used his mirror to check myself out and thought that the briefs looked good on me. I was thankful that I had shaven my lower parts off the other day, since otherwise the tight briefs meant that pubic hair would be showing out at the top.

Mike already had the cold ones and the pizza box open before I reached the hot tub in his backyard. When I got there, though, he got up and said, "I'm going to change my suit for something more fitting for the moment. Just relax and drink your cold one in the meantime."

I drank half of the can and ate some pizza slices while Mike was always; all of that dirt moving made me incredibly thirsty and hungry. Even though the briefs were a bit tight, I still felt very comfortable inside the hot tub.

Mike came back minutes later wearing a pair of white briefs just like the one I was wearing. *Where did that pair of blue briefs come from?* I asked myself, since I had seen just white ones in his bedroom when I went upstairs.

His cock and scrotum were probably bigger than mine, or his pair of briefs was smaller than the one I was wearing, since I could notice very clearly both of them fighting very hard to come out. Other than that, the briefs fit nicely on him and helped to delineate his athletic legs.

Meanwhile, his exposed hairy chest sported some bulgy and nice pair of pink-ish nipples. Seeing him like that made me realize that he was a lot hairier than I was, and any comparisons would have been disservices to his natural attribute.

As for me, my nipples used to stand out just as much as his did. The curious thing was to see someone with similar nipples, since it gave me a view I never had before. It was quite enlightening to see those protruding fruits willing and shaking as he walked. In a way, *it turned me on...*

OTHER BICURIOUS SERIES AND MORE

SERIES - BICURIOUS GUYS

1. Caught Looking by the Quarterback
2. Caught Looking by the Basketeer
3. Caught Looking by the Dropout
4. Caught Looking by the Jock
5. Caught Looking by the Roommate

SERIES - GAY FOR BLUE COLLARS

1. Given to the Cop
2. Given to the Miner
3. Given to the Plumber
4. Given to the Firefighter
5. Given to the Mechanic

ABOUT THE AUTHOR

Steamy MM stories, baby! Michael Levi can't go a day without sitting down and putting into words all the dirty scenes that sprout in his mind. His collection is diverse, but it's gay love only. You won't find anything else on his author page. And if you are looking for something free, check his mailing list. Warning: it can be extra spicy.

When he isn't writing, he's chilling out by the lake close to his house. Nothing better than kicking back with a martini in his hand as he dreams if he'll ever find the man he wants.

www.ingramcontent.com/pod-product-compliance
Lightning Source LLC
Chambersburg PA
CBHW052138150726
48002CB00006B/2661